STORIES
TO
TELL
A CAT

STORIES TO TELL A CAT

Collected and retold by
ALVIN SCHWARTZ

Illustrated by Catherine Huerta

HarperCollins*Publishers*

To Susannah,
my cat and my friend

Stories to Tell a Cat
Text copyright © 1992 by Alvin Schwartz
Illustrations copyright © 1992 by Catherine Huerta
Typography by Al Cetta
1   2   3   4   5   6   7   8   9   10
First Edition
❖

Library of Congress Cataloging-in-Publication Data
Schwartz, Alvin, date
    Stories to tell a cat / collected by Alvin Schwartz ; illustrated by
Catherine Huerta.
        p.   cm.
    Includes bibliographical references.
    Summary: A collection of cat stories drawn from folklore, some
realistic and some fanciful.
    ISBN 0-06-020850-3. — ISBN 0-06-020851-1 (lib. bdg.)
    1. Tales.   2. Cats—Folklore.   [1. Folklore.   2. Cats—Folklore.]
I. Huerta, Catherine, ill.   II. Title.
PZ8.1.S399St   1992   91-37257
398.2—dc20   CIP
[E]   AC

Contents

BRAVE AND NOBLE CATS

Now and then I tell my cat stories about other cats. After supper, often I sit in my big green chair and turn down the lights, and she climbs onto my lap, and we begin.

She has heard all the stories in this book, and many other stories, too. I have told her tales of brave and noble cats, of foolish cats and scary cats, of cats who were mighty hunters and others who were a big nuisance.

As I tell her about their experiences, she peers into the darkness through half-closed eyes, as if she can see it all taking place before her.

Why do I tell stories to my cat? It is a nice cozy way to spend an evening—sitting there with that furry creature on your lap, telling tales you like. Besides, cats like hearing about adventures that they might have one day. Ask any cat.

ALVIN SCHWARTZ

STORIES
TO
TELL
A CAT

Rosie and Arthur

One day a kitten came around the corner and moved into Rosie's house. Rosie called him Arthur.

Arthur was the smallest, skinniest cat Rosie had ever seen. On the other hand, Rosie was the biggest, fattest girl Arthur had ever seen. She was only ten years old, but she was a mountain of a girl.

"If Arthur eats what I eat, he will grow," she thought. "He will be nice and plump like me."

Rosie shared all her meals with Arthur. She gave him hamburgers, hot dogs, tacos, fried chicken, French fried potatoes, chocolate marshmallow cookies, and everything else she liked to eat.

It is not the kind of food that is good for a kitten, but Arthur loved it. The more he ate, the bigger he grew. And the bigger he grew, the more he ate. He never seemed to have enough.

Rosie liked Arthur. Whenever he wanted something to eat, she always tried to find something special for him. But one Saturday when Arthur came into the kitchen for a snack, there was very little to eat. All Rosie could find was some raspberry ripple ice cream. After he ate that, Arthur wanted more. But that's all there was. He looked deep into Rosie's eyes and whined.

"Be patient," Rosie said. "Mother has gone to the supermarket. She'll be back soon."

"I am starving," Arthur thought, "and she tells me to be patient." He rubbed against one of Rosie's legs and purred. But it didn't do any good. She was busy cutting up vegetables for dinner and ignored him. He whined again, but she paid no attention.

Arthur went back to his bowl. He sniffed at it. He ran his tongue around the inside. It still was empty. He stared at Rosie. She looked so big and juicy—and delicious. He would eat *her*! Since he was starving to death, he was sure she wouldn't mind.

Arthur crept forward silently, as if he were stalking a mouse. When Rosie looked up and smiled at him, he stopped. When she turned back to the vegetables, he crept

forward again. Except for the knife striking the cutting board, there wasn't a sound.

Suddenly Arthur jumped at Rosie, but he was so big and clumsy, he missed. "What are you doing?" Rosie shouted at him. "What's wrong with you?" When he tried again, she jumped up on the kitchen table. When he tried a third time, she climbed up on top of the refrigerator and screamed for help. But no one else was home.

Then Arthur jumped once more. This time he landed right next to her. "Get off!" she shrieked, and tried to push him away. He opened his mouth wide. She felt his breath on her face, his rough tongue on her skin.

She woke up. There was Arthur, no bigger than a kitten, sitting on her chest, licking her, whining for something to eat.

If you were a cat,
And I was a cat,
We'd both be cats together.
And when the sun went down,
And the moon came up,
We'd climb a tree,
Just you and me,
And we'd howl and yowl,
And scratch and scream,
Then close our eyes—
And dream.

The Nest

There was an old man who lived all alone. His only company was a family of mice that had a nest in a hole behind the kitchen stove. Just a few mice lived there when he moved in, but now there were thirty or forty of them.

When people have mice, usually they get a cat to drive them away. But mice didn't bother this man. Their comings and goings kept him from feeling lonely.

When the man died, someone with a cat moved in. Soon after, one of the mice dashed through the mousehole into the nest.

"There is a furry animal out there," the mouse said. "It looks gentle enough, but it is awfully big." Most of the mice had lived in the house all their lives. They had never seen another creature, except for the old man.

"It sounds like a cat," one of the older mice said. "It

may look gentle, but it is not. If we are not careful, it will eat every one of us."

The next day a mouse on its way back from the attic came upon the cat. It towered above him like some ancient monster. Instead of running, the mouse stopped and stared at it. He watched spellbound as the cat leaped into the air, bared its claws, and plunged down at him. He dodged, and raced for the mousehole.

"The cat almost killed me," he cried.

"The next time you won't be so lucky," the old mouse said. "He'll strike you with his paw, then kick you this way and that like a soccer ball. When he gets tired of playing with you, he'll bite off your head and eat you. It has happened to others."

The next day two mice went out to search for food and did not come back. In the days that followed three more did not return. They lay in the cat's stomach, slowly dissolving.

After that the mice stayed in their nest. For the first time in their lives they were afraid. Only when they were hungry did they go out, and only when they were sure the cat was not there. They had become prisoners.

The cat soon realized that the mice were hiding from him. "I will have to trick them into coming out," he

thought. "I will pretend that I am dead. Then they will come."

There was a large curtain in the living room, with a pair of drawstrings to open and close it. When the owners of the house were away, the cat climbed to the top of the curtain. He stuck his back feet into the drawstrings and hung there upside down, his head dangling, his eyes closed.

A mouse who had been searching for food saw him. The mouse stopped and stared in amazement. "The cat looks dead," he thought. "The people must have punished him for eating mice. He is dead!"

He raced back to the nest. "THE CAT IS DEAD!" he shouted. "He doesn't move. He is dead! Come and see!"

"It could be a trick," the old mouse said. "Stay here. I'll go and see." He crept through the mousehole and looked into the living room. There was the cat hanging from the drawstrings, just as the young mouse had said. "He does look dead," the old mouse thought. "But it is hard to be sure." He waited a few minutes more. The cat still did not move.

The old mouse went back to the nest. "He does look dead," he said. The mice burst into cheers and ran to see for themselves. "Of course, it could be a trick," the old mouse added. But by then, no one was there to hear him.

The cat was still hanging from the drawstrings. "He is dead!" the mice cried. "He is dead, dead, dead!" In their joy they began to dance. As they swept around and around, the cat let go of the drawstrings and dropped to the floor. He pounced on one mouse after another. Before they knew it, six or seven had found their way into his stomach.

The others raced back to the nest. They crowded around the old mouse. "Unless we do something," he said, "he will eat us all."

"Let's leave," one of the mice said. "We will gnaw through the back wall and go somewhere else."

"This is our home," another said. "Our family has lived here for years. Why should *we* leave? We were here first. That disgusting cat should leave."

"We could tell the new owners that the cat must go," another said.

"When they see us coming, they'll run," one of the mice replied. "For some reason we frighten them."

"We could kill the cat," someone else said. "We could attack him, as if we were an army."

"That's impossible," the old mouse said. "He is too big, too smart, too fast for a mouse to kill—even thirty mice. He would kill us all in a minute."

A young mouse stood up. "There is a bell in the kitchen," he said. "It is a small bell with a string on it. We could hang it around the cat's neck. When he moves, the bell will tinkle. We will always know where he is."

Everyone cheered.

"That is a wonderful idea," the old mouse said. "The bell will save us. Now who will hang it around the cat's neck?"

No one answered.

The Green Chicken

Jill's friend left his parrot, Edward, with her for a few days. She put Edward's perch in a sunny window in the kitchen. It was a pleasant place for him to rest. She fastened a long, thin chain to one of his legs so that he could fly when he wanted to, but could not fly away.

Edward had learned to speak a few words his owners had taught him. "Good morning!" he would croak. "Have you had your breakfast yet? Have a bit of buttered toast. It's awfully good."

But at Jill's house Edward had nothing to say. He sat quietly on his perch looking this way and that, his big golden eyes peering sadly out of his bright green feathers.

"What is that hairy thing in the corner?" he asked himself.

It was Jill's cat, Beatrice, staring at him. "Whatever can

[15]

that be?" Beatrice thought. "Oh, of course. It is a green chicken. How delicious it looks!"

Edward stared back at Beatrice. "That is an enemy," he told himself. He ruffled his feathers, rattled his chain, tapped his bill nervously on his perch, and waited.

Beatrice crept out of the corner, her body pressed to the floor, her tiny yellow eyes fixed on Edward. Edward watched anxiously, raising first one foot, then the other.

Suddenly Beatrice sprang into the air and landed right next to him.

"Good morning," Edward cried out in fright. "Have you had your breakfast yet?"

Beatrice was so startled she fell off the perch and landed on her head.

"Have a piece of buttered toast," Edward croaked. "It's awfully good."

"It's *not* a green chicken," Beatrice thought. "It's a green *person!*" She ran from the room and did not go near Edward again.

The Big Rat

Like most rats, this one was the color of mud, with yellow pointed teeth, blood-colored eyes, and a long leathery tail. But it was no ordinary rat. It was over two feet long and as fat as a pig.

The rat came out of the cornfield and went into the kitchen. It trotted quickly across the room and leaped up onto the table where Ben and Maureen and their children were eating supper. It walked from dish to dish, sniffing at their food and squeaking.

Maureen and the children ran out of the house. Ben grabbed a frying pan and slammed it down, hard, on the rat's head. The rat bared its teeth and came at him. Scared out of his wits, Ben fled. The rat ate all the food on the table and left.

"That was a terrible thing," said Ben. "But the rat's gone now. We'll never see it again." He was mistaken. While they were eating breakfast the next morning, the rat returned. It jumped up onto the table, stuck its snout into their food, and began eating. Once more they ran.

"We'll get a cat," said Ben. "If we had a cat, a rat wouldn't come near us."

They tried all the farms nearby. Finally they found a cat that seemed right. It was a black cat named Jane. "She's on the young side," her owner said. "But she's strong, and she's vicious with rats, just vicious." So they bought Jane and took her home.

While they were eating supper that night, the rat came back. Everyone ran. Jane took one look at the monster and fled, too. The rat ate everything on the table and left. But even after it was gone, Jane did not come back.

From then on, the rat was there for every meal. Ben and his family gave up eating in the kitchen. They ate in the attic, in the basement, in the barn, anywhere they thought they could eat in peace. But the rat always found them and took their food. They didn't know what to do.

One night they heard a cat outside. When Ben opened the door, Jane walked in. Behind her was another cat. It could have been her twin, except that this cat was as big as the rat, maybe bigger.

The two cats sat by the fire. They washed themselves and took a nap. Watching them gave Ben courage. "I am tired of hiding from that rat," he told Maureen. "Tomorrow we are going to eat our breakfast at the kitchen table where *we* belong."

They were eating there the next morning when the rat returned. When it saw them, it stopped. "Why aren't they in the attic or the basement where they belong?" it thought. "What is going on?"

Then it saw the big cat. The cat stretched and yawned and twirled its tail. It walked slowly toward the rat. The family got out as fast as it could. And so did Jane.

The rat raced across the kitchen and threw itself at the cat. The cat pounced on the rat. Over the table and under the chairs they went, up onto the counters and into the sink, biting, scratching, shrieking, screaming.

The cat fled from the house with the rat right behind. Up and down the yard they fought, then into the cornfield, and out into the road. First one was on top, then the other. Then one broke loose, with the other right behind. Screams of anger and shrieks of pain filled the air. Blood, fur, and dust were everywhere.

Ben, Maureen, and the children watched with bulging

eyes as the big rat and the big cat fought on and on. Meanwhile, Jane sat on a branch in a tree washing herself.

As night approached, the cat struck the rat a terrible blow with its paw. It knocked the rat to the ground, where it lay without moving.

In the dying light it was hard to be sure. But it looked to Ben as if the cat leaped into the air and raised its left paw in triumph. Then it vanished. And so did Jane.

The Fastest Cat on Earth

The cat we are about to meet is the fastest cat on earth. He is a regular whirlwind. He is so fast he can out-run anyone or anything. At least that is what he says.

The fastest cat on earth was lying in a meadow, half

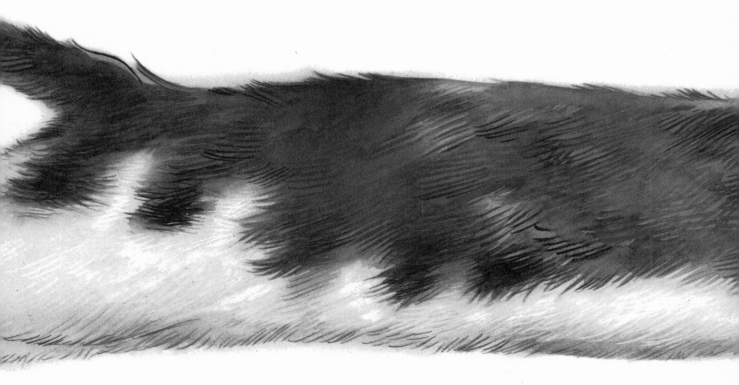

dozing in the hot sun. He was waiting for a mouse or a young rabbit to go by, or even a butterfly—anything he could chase and catch and eat. But nothing stirred. It was very boring.

Then he saw a crab scurrying toward the beach in that weird way in which crabs move, its ten skinny legs all going like crazy.

"I *hate* crabmeat," the cat thought. "But maybe that crab and I could have a race. I would win, of course, but at least it would be something to do.

"Hey, crab," he called. "Do you want to race? It would be fun."

"It would be fun for you," the crab said in its tiny voice. "You're faster than me." It paused. "Of course, I'm smarter than you. Okay. I'll do it."

"We'll race down the path to that tree," the cat said. "On your mark, get set—go!"

When the fastest cat on earth leaped forward, the crab grabbed the cat's tail and hung on tight. He weighed so little, the cat didn't even know he was there. The cat tore down the path as quickly as he could, with the crab dangling behind him.

Just before the cat reached the tree, he stopped, turned around, and looked back. The crab was nowhere in sight. But while the cat was peering back down the path, the crab quietly dropped to the ground and scurried across the finish line.

"I knew I would beat him," the cat thought. "But not this easily. Of course, I *am* the fastest cat on earth. Yet he does have *ten* legs." Then he heard a tiny voice.

"Hey, cat," the voice called. "I win!"

When the cat saw the crab, he could not believe his eyes. "You win?" he said. "When did you pass me? I didn't see you anywhere."

"You didn't?" said the crab. "Why, I was right behind you the whole way."

The Make-Believe Cats

Unlike his brothers, Paul could not do his share of the work on the farm. He was too frail. But oh, how he could draw. He would sit under a tree and make one picture after another. He drew everything he saw. But mostly he drew cats.

There were dozens of cats on his father's farm. He made pictures of them eating, stretching, running, climbing, walking, sitting, washing, hunting, even killing. He thought they were the most beautiful creatures he had ever seen.

"This farm is no place for Paul," his mother told his father. "He is not strong enough for this sort of work. He'll get sick."

So his father found Paul a job with a grocer a few miles

away. The boy did whatever was needed, and in his free time he drew cats. They reminded him of home.

One day he drew a big cat on a wall in the store. The cat was eating a fish, the same kind the store sold. He thought the grocer would be pleased. Instead, he made Paul scrub it off and fired him.

The boy was too ashamed to go home. He wandered around the countryside, finding work wherever he could. Then Paul heard that some monks needed help with the cooking and cleaning at their monastery.

He arrived toward dusk. When he knocked, no one answered. He tried the door. It opened into a large empty hall that was growing dark. Paul called out, "Hello!"—but no one replied.

"They must have gone into town," he thought. "I'll wait." He lay down on the floor and tried to sleep. But in this strange empty place, far from home, he was too restless to sleep.

"Since I can't sleep, I will draw," he thought. In the shadows he saw a tall paper screen that separated one part of the room from another. Often such screens had beautiful pictures on them. But this screen was blank.

Paul found a piece of charcoal in the fireplace and drew three large black-and-white cats on the screen. He drew them sitting in a circle, staring at one another. When he finished, he fell asleep.

During the night something awakened him. He could not hear or see anything. Yet he knew that something was there in the hall with him. It frightened him. But he was so tired, he fell asleep again.

When he awakened the next morning, he could not believe what he saw. Dead rats were everywhere. Then the screen on which he had drawn the three cats caught his eye. He had drawn them sitting in a circle, staring at one another. Now they were standing, looking right at him. Their mouths and their claws were red with blood.

He threw the dead rats into the woods. Then he dipped his shirt in water and gently washed the blood from the picture. Afterward he touched the screen, to make sure he hadn't damaged it—but instead of feeling like paper, it felt like cat's fur.

Paul heard the sound of purring. "There's a cat outside," he told himself. But when he went to look, there was no cat.

He walked to the nearby village, and there he found the monks. They said that a plague of rats had driven them from the monastery. Paul told them the rats were dead, but that he didn't know what had killed them.

When Paul went back to the monastery with the monks he showed them his drawing. The cats were again sitting in a circle staring at one another. Paul never did tell the monks what he thought had happened. They would not have believed it anyway.

Paul lived with the monks for many years, cooking and cleaning for them. In his free time he drew pictures. He drew everything he saw. But mostly he drew cats.

The tall paper screen still stood in the hall, and the cats on the screen still sat in a circle staring at one another. Now and then they stood and stared at him. And now and then he heard a cat purring. But no one else ever noticed.

There once
were two cats of Kilkenny.
Each thought
there was one cat too many.
So they fought
and they fit,
and they scratched
and they bit until,
except for their tails
and the tips of their nails,
instead of two cats,
there weren't any.

The Ship's Cat

The *Mary Anne* was a small freighter that sailed up and down the coast carrying cargo from one city to another. When a sailor named Stump Smith joined the crew, he brought along his cat, Henrietta.

From her first day on board, Henrietta went everywhere on that ship. She prowled the decks, sat in the lifeboats, slept in the cabins. She explored the engine room, the hold, and the galley, where the cook saved all kinds of leftovers for her. She ate like a queen.

Soon everyone thought of Henrietta as the ship's cat.

There was also a ship's dog on board, a big Irish setter named Patrick. He was the captain's dog. Dogs and cats do not always get along. But Patrick and Henrietta got along fine. They ate together and even lay in the sun together.

Whenever the *Mary Anne* came into a port, some of the

crew went ashore at night to see the sights. So did Henrietta, but she was always back the next morning.

One day while they were sailing from one city to another, Stump could not find Henrietta. He looked in all her favorite haunts, but there was no sign of her. Finally he looked under his bunk. There she was, with three new kittens.

Henrietta spent all her time with them. She licked them clean, and sheltered them from cold drafts with her body. She moved them when they were uncomfortable, and helped them as they began to crawl and walk. She never left them for a minute.

When the kittens were a month old, the *Mary Anne* was tied up at a wharf in a large city. The crew had unloaded the cargo and had stored a new one in the hold. Late that afternoon some of the sailors went ashore. "We sail early tomorrow," the captain told them. "Don't forget."

Henrietta had not been off the ship since her kittens were born. When she heard the sailors leaving, she left the kittens under the bunk and went ashore, just as she used to do before they were born.

When Stump found that she was gone, he sighed. "She'll be back tomorrow, like always," he thought. He got some milk from the galley and fed the kittens. He held them for a while. Then he crawled into bed for a nap. They snuggled against him.

After Henrietta left the ship, she went down one block, then two more. At the next corner she smelled, then saw, a cart filled with fish. Next to it stood a peddler. She grabbed a fish and ran off with it.

"Thief!" the peddler screamed. Henrietta paid no attention. She dashed into an alley, dropped her prize, and began to eat it. Suddenly, a tomcat twice Henrietta's size appeared and grabbed the fish. Screaming like a banshee, Henrietta hurled herself at him, but he shook her off, ran from the alley, and was gone.

By now the streetlights had come on, and heavy clouds had begun dropping rain. Henrietta crawled under a car parked at the curb, to keep from getting wet. She dozed until the barking of a dog awakened her. The dog was peering at her from the sidewalk. It was too big to get at her. Instead it ran around and around the car barking.

One of the car doors opened and slammed shut. The motor roared, and the car drove off. Henrietta and the big dog stood staring at one another. When the dog jumped at her, Henrietta ran down the street and up a tree to safety.

By now Henrietta was very hungry. Except for one bite

of fish, she had eaten nothing since leaving the ship. The smell of food cooking drifted into the tree. Henrietta backed down the tree and followed her nose. It led her through the back door of a restaurant, into a kitchen, and up onto a wooden counter, where chickens, steaks, and other foods were being prepared. She sat down next to a plump chicken and began chewing on one of its legs.

Suddenly there were angry shouts. A meat cleaver struck the counter like a guillotine only an inch from her nose. Henrietta raced from the kitchen into the alley, then dodged across a busy street into the darkness of a park. She climbed another tree, curled up into a ball of fur, and purred softly to calm her nerves.

Soon she heard music. A young man and a young woman had sat down under Henrietta's tree and turned on a cassette player. Soon they were hugging and kissing. "Oh, Jason," she murmured. "Oh, Julie," he murmured back.

After a meat cleaver, a dog, and a tomcat, what Henrietta needed was peace and quiet, not music and kissing. She jumped out of the tree and was walking slowly toward some shrubs when an arm reached out and grabbed her. She screeched and tried to break away, but Jason held on tight.

The young woman pointed a flashlight at Henrietta. "What a pretty kitty," she said. She patted Henrietta's head.

"Let's keep her," said Jason.

Henrietta snarled and sank her teeth deep into Jason's hand. Jason screeched with pain. The cat leaped from his arms and hid under a bush. After a while she fell asleep.

When the first streaks of red appeared in the sky, birds all over the park began chattering. Henrietta sat up. She felt restless, as if she needed to be on her way to somewhere. A garter snake crawled by. She trapped it with a paw and ate it. She looked for something else to eat, a bird or a mole, but there was nothing nearby.

She walked out of the park, following the scent of the trail she had left the night before. The farther she went, the more she recalled where she was going.

By the time the sun was halfway into the sky, Henrietta had found her way back to the wharf. But the *Mary Anne* and Henrietta's kittens no longer were there. The captain had waited and waited for her, but he could not wait any longer. "We'll be back in a few weeks," he told Stump. "Maybe we'll find her then."

Henrietta walked slowly to the end of the wharf. There were other ships tied up, but not her ship. She found a

quiet place and washed herself. She waited patiently all day, but the *Mary Anne* did not return.

That night Henrietta went into the city again. The next morning she came back to the wharf. The ship still was not there. Each night she went off on her own. Each morning she returned and waited.

Three weeks later the *Mary Anne* slowly made its way up the river. Henrietta watched as the ship moved toward the wharf, not knowing if it was her ship or some other. When it got close enough, the captain's dog Patrick saw Henrietta and began barking. Then Stump and the rest of the crew saw her. Henrietta recognized them. She quivered with excitement.

To the cheers of the crew, she leaped from the wharf to the ship's deck. Her kittens, now young cats, stared at her, not sure who she was. Later they would remember her. Now, when she ran to them, they backed off, hissing and spitting.

But, of course, Patrick knew her. He dashed here and there barking with excitement. Then, with his big, wet tongue, he licked her face.

The Cat Came Back

Rebecca was a dreadful cat. She hid dead mice in the cookie jar. She left her hairs in the toothpaste. She hung from the lights in the ceiling. And after everyone was asleep, she walked on the piano keys and sang.

Rebecca's owners tried to get her to change her ways, but she wouldn't. So they gave her to a family out in the country. They pretended to be sad to see her go. But they were VERY glad. "No more Rebecca!" they told one another, and they laughed.

But Re - bec - ca came back, She would-n't stay a-way,

She was peek- ing in the wind- ow The ve-ry next day.

So they gave her to a man who was going way down east. They told him to leave her with the one he liked the least. "See you in a hundred years!" they called.

But Re - bec - ca came back, She would-n't stay a-way,

She was bang - ing on the door The ve-ry next day.

So they gave her to a sailor who was on his way to
Spain. But his ship went down in a very heavy rain.

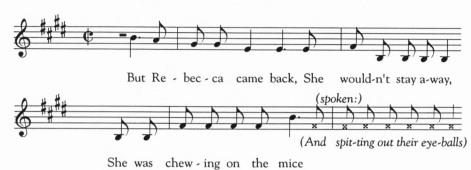

But Re - bec - ca came back, She would-n't stay a-way,

(spoken:)

(And spit-ting out their eye-balls)

She was chew - ing on the mice

The ve-ry next day.

So they gave her to a woman who was going up in a bal-loon. They asked her to leave Rebecca with the man in the moon. "Good-bye forever!" they cried.

But Re - bec - ca came back, She would-n't stay a-way,

She was screech-ing down the chim-ney The ve - ry next day.

So they gave up. And Rebecca stayed and stayed. And each year her behavior got worse and worse. Then one day, after many years, she died of old age. Her owners were sad to see anyone die. But when Rebecca's turn came, they did not seem too unhappy. "How sad," they said, and they danced a jig.

But _____ Re-bec-ca's ghost came back, It would-n't stay a-way,

It   drift-ed through the door The   ve-ry next day.

Deep in the Swamp

It was dark when I finished with work. So I decided to take a shortcut home. I was tired and hungry, and it would save a lot of time.

I took an old trail into the woods. Then, by the light of the moon, I headed into the swamp, stepping from one foot log to the next to keep from getting wet.

A bat slipped by. An owl hooted, then stopped. It was so quiet, I could hear myself breathing. Suddenly a bullfrog hit the water with a big splash. I stood for a minute and watched him swim away, his wet green skin glistening in the moonlight. When I started moving again, I looked up and saw a big black cat waiting at the end of the log, bigger than a cat should be. Come from out of nowhere, hair all on end, eyes like fire.

"Beat it!" I hollered. He didn't move an inch. I grabbed

a stick, smacked him with it hard as I could. It went *right through him* like he wasn't there. Yet there he was, staring at me with those big red eyes!

"Got to get out of here," I thought. I hurried back toward the woods, hopping from log to log fast as I could go. After a while I figured I was free and clear. Then I saw him waiting up ahead, bigger than before. When he came toward me, I turned tail and ran back into the swamp.

"If I keep moving, I'll make it all the way," I told myself. But the cat was waiting there, too, bigger still, his tail twitching and twisting like a giant snake ready to strike. Wherever I turned, he was waiting, those fiery eyes burning holes in the dark. Then all of a sudden he was gone.

I ran for the woods again. I tripped, fell into the water, climbed out, kept going. He was right behind me. I could feel it. When I got to the edge of the swamp, I looked back. There he was, watching every move I made. But this time he stayed put.

Maybe he just wanted me to know whose swamp it was. I know now. I don't go that way anymore.

The King of the Cats

"I'm going for a walk in the woods," Joe said. "I'll be back soon." But Joe didn't get back until long after dark.

"Where have you been?" his father asked. "We were worried about you."

"I got lost," said Joe. "I was on my way home when one of those heavy mists came down from the hills. I couldn't see where I was going, and I took a wrong turn. I didn't know where I was."

Joe's cat, Richard, came over and rubbed against his leg. He leaned over and scratched the cat's neck. "It was weird," Joe said. "It was like something I dreamed.

"I walked and walked until, finally, I saw a light way off in the distance. At first I thought it was from a house. But as I got closer, I realized that there was no house, that the light was coming from the top of a big old hollow tree.

"There was no one in sight. There wasn't a sound. Yet here was this light pouring out of a tree in the middle of the woods in the middle of the night. I scrambled to the top to see what was inside."

Just then Richard curled up on the floor next to where Joe was sitting and lay there watching him.

"Look at Richard," Joe said. "I bet he knows what I'm saying."

"Forget Richard," his father said impatiently. "Tell us what you saw."

"I saw a church," Joe said. "I was looking down into a small church. Right below me there was an altar with candles burning on it. And in front of the altar there was an empty grave, waiting for a body.

"I heard weeping and wailing. Then a funeral came into the church with a small black coffin. On top of the coffin there was a tiny gold crown."

Richard sat straight up and stared at him.

Joe was silent for a minute. "The strangest part," he said, "was that cats were carrying the coffin—six cats walking on their hind legs!

"Another cat, bigger than the rest, walked in front. A smaller cat, covered from head to foot with a black veil,

walked behind. She was sobbing as if her heart was broken."

Suddenly Richard jumped to his feet. "So old William is dead," he said softly. Then he cried out, "Now I'm king of the cats!"

With that, he shot up the chimney and was never seen again.

Whenever one cat becomes king, another is chosen to replace him when he dies, or so it is said. This future king might be an ordinary house cat or a street cat, a mongrel or a purebred. It could be your cat.

Of course, no one ever thinks of this cat as a future king. Only those who chose him know how important he is. But when the king of the cats dies, the new king always learns of it somehow and quickly leaves to ascend the throne.

Once There Was a Cat

Once there was a cat who would appear or disappear whenever it wanted to. It was there. Then it was gone. Then it was there again, and gone again, depending on its mood.

Sometimes the cat vanished all at once. At other times it disappeared more gradually. It would start disappearing at the tip of its tail. Then, bit by bit, the rest of its body would fade away, until nothing was left but a grin.

And finally that was gone, until the next time.
Meow!

A TAIL OF GRASS

How did this mysterious, elegant, cruel, playful, lovable creature we call a cat come to be? There are many stories.

Some say that a goddess in India created the cat when rats and mice invaded her country and there was no animal to deal with them. She dug some clay, added water, and kneaded the clay like dough, then formed it into the body of a small animal about the size of a loaf of bread.

She added four legs and a head, then two pointed ears, a mouth and a nose. She snatched two fireflies out of the evening sky for her cat to use as eyes.

So that it could kill rats and mice, she turned the bits of silver on her bracelet into claws. So that it could jump more easily, she plucked a handful of long grasses from a field, twisted them tightly together, and added a tail.

Then she asked her husband to hold still. From his stiff white beard, she pulled two dozen hairs. She placed some above the cat's eyes, and others on its cheeks and around its mouth, so that it could better guide itself through tall grass while hunting.

Having done all this, she was disappointed. This cat looked more like a rat than a master of rats. She stuck her fingers into the soot at the bottom of an old fire and drew black lines on its body. Then she found red clay and added more color here and there. Now the cat looked like a cat, not a rat.

The goddess held the cat in her arms admiring it. To give it life, she breathed on it. It opened its eyes and purred. "It is praying to me," she thought, and she smiled. At that moment the cat leaped from her arms and pounced on a rat, just as it was meant to do.

Others say that the cat was created during an emergency aboard Noah's ark. As that story goes, Noah found that a mouse, actually the Devil in disguise, had gnawed a hole through the hull of the ark. If the mouse kept on that way, the vessel would sink, and Noah and his family and all the animals on board would drown.

When Noah told the animals about the problem, the lion sneezed. Out of its nose flew a small cat. The cat ate the mouse and saved the ark.

Scientists today tell another story. They say that the cat did not appear in a single moment, but developed and changed over tens of millions of years. They believe that cats we would recognize appeared about 35 million years ago. These were big cats, like today's lions and tigers. Then other species evolved, including the small cats that are the heroes and heroines of this book.

Ancient Egypt seems to have been the first place where many people had house cats. This was about four thousand years ago. At that time cats were treated with great respect and honor. One reason, of course, was that they killed rats and mice. But they also were admired for their beauty and grace, their dignified behavior, their cleanliness, and the many children they had.

When a cat or kitten died, it was mummified and preserved in a mummy case shaped like a cat. The people with whom it lived shaved their eyebrows in mourning.

The oldest picture we have of a house cat was found inside a tomb in Thebes, Egypt. The cat wore gold earrings. Its name was Bouhaki.

NOTES

The publications cited are described in the Bibliography.

Rosie and Arthur. There are stories of monster cats told in most countries. Some of these casts are magical. But others just love to eat, and the more they eat, the more they grow. And the bigger they get, the more frightening they become.

The tale of Rosie and Arthur is based loosely on two such stories. One is a scary camp story that I heard while growing up in New York State of a cat who tries to eat its master. The other is a Norwegian folktale called "The Greedy Cat" or "The Fat Cat." During one remarkable day this cat ate a man, a woman, and their child; two bears and their bear cub; seven other animals; a bride and a groom and their wedding party; and a funeral procession.

When the cat also tried to eat a billy goat, the goat butted her in the stomach. She burst open and everyone escaped. See Asbjornsen, pp. 33–41.

A Virginia story, "Sody Sallyratús," involves a bear instead of a cat. See Chase, pp. 81–87. Garrison Keillor, the writer and performer, told a story somewhat like "Rosie and Arthur" on one of his 1985 "Prairie Home Companion" programs.

If You Were a Cat. This rhyme was inspired by another that was popular on college campuses in the United States in the 1930s. It went:

> If I were a cat,
> And you were a cat,
> And we all were cats together—
> We'd stroll on a fence,
> Where the shrubbery is dense,
> In rainy or other weather.

See Wells, p. 134.

The Nest. This story is an expanded version of "Belling

the Cat," one of the Aesop fables. The strategy used by the cat in overcoming the mice is from another fable, "The Cat and the Old Rat," that the French fabulist and poet Jean de La Fontaine wrote in the seventeenth century.

Most fables in the Western world are called Aesop's fables, although there is no clear proof that Aesop existed or, if he did, that he wrote them. According to legend, he was a slave in Greece around 570 B.C. who was freed because of his great wisdom. It is thought that some fables bearing his name were Greek folktales that he or someone else adapted. "Belling the Cat" was one of these.

The fables attributed to Aesop were translated into Latin around A.D. 100 by the Greek writer Phaedrus, then were retold two hundred years later by the Roman poet Babrius. Those we know today are based on their work. See Leach, *Dictionary*, pp. 17–18; Jacobs, *Aesop*, pp. v–vi, 167–174.

The Green Chicken. This story is based on an encounter that a cat owned by the French poet Théophile Gautier had with a visiting parrot. Although the cat's name is Beatrice in our story, her real name was Madame Théophile. She was a reddish cat with a white breast, blue eyes, and a pink nose. See Repplier, pp. 202–207.

[61]

The Big Rat. This story is based loosely on an Irish folk-tale recorded in County Galway in 1938. See O'Sullivan, pp. 189–191.

The Fastest Cat on Earth. This tale is based on a Japanese version of the Aesop fable of the tortoise and the hare. In the Aesop story there is no trickery, only the persistence of a tortoise winning out over the silly boasting of a hare. See Seki, p. 25.

The Make-Believe Cats. This story is adapted and expanded from a Japanese folktale I have known since childhood. For a related version, see Belting, pp. 83–89.

Tall tales in which paintings are so realistic that they come alive are found in American folklore. These include stories of artists who paint dogs that bite, cannons that go off, and snowstorms that cause people to catch cold. See Schwartz, pp. 42, 112.

There Once Were Two Cats of Kilkenny. This is a traditional tale about the town of Kilkenny in southern Ireland. It is said to be based on bitter hatred the English and the Irish who lived there had for one another during the Middle Ages. Various sources.

The Ship's Cat. There are many cats like Henrietta who wander into unfamiliar territory and find their way home with the help of a scent trail they have left. There are others who have been taken long distances from home by car or train and, with no scent trail to follow, also find their way back. No one can explain how this is possible, but there are many accounts of this kind. See Repplier, pp. 247–253.

The best-known such story, however, is fiction. It is a novel for young people called *The Incredible Journey*, in which a cat and two dogs who had been left with friends travel 250 miles through the wilderness to return home. See Burnford.

"The Ship's Cat" is adapted and expanded from a true story in Repplier of an oil tanker that ran between Savona, Italy, and Philadelphia.

The Cat Came Back. This is a song that was written by one person, yet became part of our folklore as people added lyrics of their own over the years. The original lyrics were written in 1893 by Henry S. Miller for a minstrel song. Soon there were dozens of versions of how the cat's owner tried to get rid of it.

The cat was given to a cyclist who was on his way

around the world and disappeared. It was locked in a safe, then shipped away on a train that crashed. It was carried off by a cyclone. It was even caught in the blast of an atomic bomb. But each time it came back with nine more lives.

In following this tradition, I changed some incidents and added others of my own. I also changed the refrain somewhat. It often is sung in this way:

But the cat came back the very next day,
The cat came back, they thought it was a goner;
But the cat came back for it couldn't stay away.

The music in the text was adapted by Barbara Carmer Schwartz.

See Spaeth, p. 166; Randolph, pp. 198–200; Ipcar's children's picture book is based on this song.

Deep in the Swamp. The cat in this story is a "plat-eye," the ghost of a person who was not buried properly. The ghost returns as an animal, often a dog, that gets larger and larger. If someone stares too long at its fiery eyes, he or she may be swallowed by them, it is said.

"The Swamp Cat" is drawn from a number of "plat-eye" stories in the southeastern United States. See Peterkin, pp. 209–210; Puckett, p. 130; Davis, p. 248; Gonzales, p. 183.

The King of the Cats. This unusual variant of "The King of the Cats" was adapted from an English folktale in Hartland, pp. 126–127. The most common version involves a man on his way home through the woods who comes upon a funeral procession of cats. One of the cats calls to him, "Tell Tom Tildrum that Tim Tildrum is dead." [The names change from story to story.] When the man gets home, he tells his wife what happened. Their cat cries out, "Then I'm the king of the cats!" and disappears up the chimney.

Versions of this story have been collected throughout northern Europe and in the United States. The writer Stephen Vincent Benét used the tale as the basis of a story in which an orchestra conductor performing in New York turns out to be the king of the cats and runs off with a princess who is actually a Siamese cat. See Benét, pp. 398–412.

"The King of the Cats" first appeared in English over four hundred years ago, but it was old even then. The folklorist Archer Taylor found that it was related to this story told fifteen hundred years earlier about the death of the Greek god Pan:

> As a ship sailed from Greece to Italy, it passed the island of Paxos. Those on board heard a voice from the island cry out, "Thamus, Thamus," which was the name of the ship's pilot. After Thamus replied, the voice thundered, "When you come to Palodes, tell them that the Great Pan is dead."
>
> When his ship passed Palodes, Thamus shouted, "The Great Pan is dead!" Suddenly the sound of weeping and wailing swept across the island.

See Hudson, pp. 225–231.

Once There Was a Cat. This is, of course, the famous Cheshire Cat that Lewis Carroll describes in *Alice's Adventures in Wonderland*, pp. 65–66, 71–75, 97–102.

Carroll does not explain why the cat grins all the time, even after it has disappeared. But people in Cheshire, England, know why. At one time, Cheshire was so prosperous, it was given special privileges by the English government. This meant many advantages for those who lived there. The cat was grinning, of course, because of all the privileges it had. In fact, the famous Cheshire cheeses are shaped like the head of a grinning cat. Various sources.

A Tail of Grass. The story of the cat who was created from clay is a traditional tale in India and among some

Indian tribes in South America. (Aarne-Thompson Motif 1815 A, creation of the tiger.) For another version, see Belting, pp. 60–62. Also see Elwin, *Middle India*, pp. 210–211, *Orissa*, p. 185.

The story of the cat sneezed forth by a lion is described in Thompson, p. 237. The information on the evolution of the cat is from various sources. Maria Leach refers to the picture of the cat Bouhaki in her book *The Lion Sneezed*, p. 5.

BIBLIOGRAPHY

Books that may be of interest to young people are marked with an asterisk (*).

Asbjornsen, Peter C. *Tales from the Field*. Trans., George Dasant. New York: G. P. Putnam's Sons, 1908. A collection of popular tales of Norway.

*Belting, Natalia M. *Cat Tales*. New York: Holt, Rinehart and Winston, 1959.

Benét, Stephen Vincent. *Selected Works of Stephen Vincent Benét*, Vol. 2. New York: Farrar & Rinehart, Inc., 1942.

*Burnford, Sheila E. *The Incredible Journey*. Boston: Little, Brown and Company, 1961.

Briggs, Katharine M. *Nine Lives: The Folklore of Cats*. New York: Pantheon Books, Inc., 1980.

*Carroll, Lewis, pseudonym of Charles Lutwidge

Dodgson. *Alice's Adventures in Wonderland*. New York: Random House, Inc., 1965.

*Chase, Richard. *Grandfather Tales*. Boston: Houghton Mifflin Company, 1948.

Dale-Green, Patricia. *Cult of the Cat*. Boston: Houghton Mifflin Company, 1963.

Davis, H. C. "Negro Folk-Lore in South Carolina." *Journal of American Folklore*, Vol. 27 (1914).

Dégh, Linda. *The Folktales of Hungary*. Chicago: University of Chicago Press, 1965.

Elwin, Verrier. *Myths of Middle India*. London: Oxford University Press, 1949.

————. *Tribal Myths of Orissa*. Bombay, 1953.

Fireman, Judy, ed. *Cat Catalog*. New York: Workman Publishing Co., 1976.

Gonzales, A. E. *The Black Border*. Columbia, S.C.: University of South Carolina Press, 1924.

Harris, Joel Chandler. *Nights with Uncle Remus: Myths and Legends of the Old Plantation*. Boston: James R. Osgood & Co., 1882.

Hartland, Edwin Sidney. *English Folk and Fairy Tales*. London: Walter Scott, Ltd., n.d.

Hudson, Arthur Palmer. "Some Versions of 'The King of the Cats.'" *Southern Folklore Quarterly*, Vol. 17 (1953).

*Ipcar, Dahlov Z. *The Cat Came Back.* New York: Alfred A. Knopf, Inc., 1971.

*Jacobs, Joseph. *The Fables of Aesop.* New York: The Macmillan Company, 1950.

*————. *More English Fairy Tales.* New York: Schocken Books, Inc., 1968.

Kutlowski, Edward. *Good Old Days,* Book 11. Danvers, Mass.: The Tower Press, 1969.

La Fontaine, Jean de. *The Fables of La Fontaine.* Trans., Marianne Moore. New York: The Viking Press, Inc., 1954.

*Leach, Maria. *The Lion Sneezed: Folktales and Myths of the Cat.* New York: Thomas Y. Crowell Company, 1977.

————, ed. *Standard Dictionary of Folklore, Mythology and Legend,* 2 vols. New York: Funk & Wagnalls, Inc., 1972.

O'Sullivan, Sean. *Folktales of Ireland.* Chicago: University of Chicago Press, 1952.

Peterkin, Julia. *Roll, Jordan, Roll.* New York: Robert A. Ballou, 1933.

Puckett, Newbell N. *Folk Beliefs of the Southern Negro.* Chapel Hill, N.C.: University of North Carolina Press, 1926.

Randolph, Vance. *Ozark Folksongs,* Vol. 3. Columbia, Mo.:

State Historical Society of Missouri, 1949.

Repplier, Agnes. *The Fireside Sphinx*. Boston: Houghton Mifflin and Company, 1901.

*Schwartz, Alvin. *Whoppers*. New York: J. B. Lippincott Company, 1975.

Seki, Keigo. *Folktales of Japan*. Chicago: University of Chicago Press, 1963.

Spaeth, Sigmund. *Read 'Em and Weep: The Songs You Forgot to Remember*. Garden City, N.Y.: Doubleday, Payne & Company, 1927.

Thompson, Stith. *The Folktale*. New York: Holt, Rinehart and Winston, 1946. Reprinted.: Berkeley, Cal., University of California Press, 1977.

Wells, Carolyn, and Louella D. Everett. *The Cat in Verse*. Boston: Little, Brown and Company, 1935.